The Tale of Chirpy Cricket

Arthur Scott Bailey

THE TALE OF CHIRPY CRICKET

I

THE FIDDLER

If Chirpy Cricket had begun to make music earlier in the summer perhaps he wouldn't have given so much time to fiddling in Farmer Green's farmyard. Everybody admitted that Chirpy was the most musical insect in the whole neighborhood. And it seemed as if he tried his hardest to crowd as much music as possible into a few weeks, though he had been silent enough during all the spring.

He had dug himself a hole in the ground, under some straw that was scattered near the barn; and every night, from midsummer on, he came out and made merry.

But in the daytime he was usually quiet as a mouse, sitting inside his hole and doing nothing at all except to wait patiently until it should be dark again, so that he might crawl forth from his hiding place and take up his music where he had left it unfinished the night before.

Somehow he always knew exactly where to begin. Although he carried no sheets of music with him, he never had to stop and wonder what note to begin on, for the reason that he always fiddled on the same one.

When rude people asked Chirpy Cricket—as they did now and then—why he didn't change his tune, he always replied that a person couldn't change anything without taking time. And since he expected to make only a short stay in Pleasant Valley he didn't want to fritter away any precious moments.

Chirpy Cricket's neighbors soon noticed that he carried his fiddle with him everywhere he went. And the curious ones asked him a question. "Why"— they inquired—"why are you forever taking your fiddle with you?"

And Chirpy Cricket reminded them that the summer would be gone almost before anybody knew it. He said that when he wanted to play a tune he didn't intend to waste any valuable time hunting for his fiddle.

Now, all that was true enough. But it was just as true that he couldn't have left his fiddle at home anyhow. Chirpy made his music with his two wings. He rubbed a file-like ridge of one on a rough part of the other. So his fiddle — if you could call it by that name — just naturally had to go wherever he did.

Cr-r-r-i! cr-r-r-i! cr-r-r-i! When that shrill sound, all on one note, rang out in the night everybody that heard it knew that Chirpy Cricket was sawing out his odd music. And the warmer the night the faster he played. He liked warm weather. Somehow it seemed to make him feel especially lively.

People who wanted to be disagreeable were always remarking in Chirpy Cricket's hearing that they hoped there would be an early frost. They thought of course he would know they were tired of his music and wished he would keep still.

But such speeches only made him fiddle the faster. "An early frost!" he would exclaim. "I must hurry if I'm to finish my summer's fiddling."

Now, Chirpy had dozens and dozens of relations living in holes of their own, in the farmyard or the fields. And the gentlemen were all musical. Like him, they were fiddlers. Somehow fiddling ran in their family. So on warm nights, during the last half of the summer, there was sure to be a Crickets' concert.

Sometimes it seemed to Johnnie Green, who lived in the farmhouse, as if Chirpy Cricket and his relations were trying to drown the songs of the musical Frog family, over in the swamp.

QUICK AND EASY

Of course Chirpy Cricket didn't spend all his time merely sitting quietly in his hole, in the daytime—and fiddling every night. Of course he had to eat. And each night he was in the habit of creeping out of his hole and gathering spears of grass in Farmer Green's yard, which he carried home with him.

He called that "doing his marketing." And it was lucky for him that he liked grass, there was so much of it to be had. All he had to do was to step outside his door; and there it was, all around him! It made housekeeping an easy matter and left him plenty of time, every night, to fiddle and frolic.

Somehow Chirpy could never go from one place to another in a slow, sober walk. He always moved by leaps, as if he felt too gay to plod along like Daddy Longlegs, for instance. Chirpy himself often remarked that he hadn't time to move slowly. And almost before he had finished speaking, as likely as not he would jump into the air and alight some distance away. It was all done so quickly that a person could scarcely see how it happened. But Chirpy Cricket said it was as easy as anything. And having leaped like that, often he would begin to shuffle his wings together the moment he landed on the ground, thereby making his shrill music.

Many of his neighbors declared that he believed a short life and a merry one was the best kind. And when they thought of Timothy Turtle, who was so old that nobody could even guess his age, and was so disagreeable and snappish that every one kept out of his way, the neighbors decided that possibly Chirpy Cricket's way was the better of the two. Anyhow, there was no doubt that Timothy Turtle believed in a long life and a grumpy one.

All Chirpy's relations were of the same mind as he. They acted as if they would rather make the nights ring with their music than do anything else. And Johnnie Green said one evening, when he heard Solomon Owl hooting over in the hemlock woods, that it was lucky there weren't as many Owls as there were Crickets in the valley.

If there were hundreds — or maybe thousands — of Owls, and they all hooted at the same time, there'd be no sleeping for anybody. At least that was Johnnie Green's opinion. And it does seem a reasonable one.

Chirpy Cricket's nearest relations all looked exactly like him. Everybody said that the Crickets bore a strong family resemblance to one another. But there were others — more distant cousins — that were quite unlike Chirpy. There were the Mole Crickets, who stayed in the ground and never, never came to the surface; and there were the Tree Crickets, who lived in the trees and fiddled re-teat! re-teat re-teat! until you might have thought they would get tired of their ditty.

But they never did. They seemed to like their music as much as Chirpy Cricket liked his cr-r-r-i! cr-r-r-i! cr-r-r-i!

III

THE BUMBLEBEE FAMILY

The farmyard was not the first place that Chirpy Cricket chose for his home. Before he dug himself a hole under the straw near the barn he had settled in the pasture. Although the cows seemed to think that the grass in the pasture belonged to them alone, Chirpy decided that there ought to be enough for him too, if he didn't eat too much.

He had been living in the pasture some time before he discovered that a very musical family had come to live next door to him. They were known as the Bumblebees; and there were dozens of them huddled into a hole long since deserted by some Woodchucks that had moved to other quarters.

Although they were said to be great workers—most of them!—the Bumblebee family found plenty of time to make music. They were very fond of humming. And in the beginning Chirpy Cricket thought their humming a pleasant sound to hear, as he sat in his dark hole during the daytime.

"They're having a party in there!" he said, the first time he noticed the droning music. "No doubt"—he added—"no doubt they're enjoying a dance!"

The thought made him feel so jolly that if it had only been dark out of doors he would have left his home and leaped about in the pasture.

All that day, between naps, Chirpy could hear the humming. "It's certainly a long party!" he exclaimed, when he awoke late in the afternoon and heard the Bumblebee family still making music. But about sunset their humming stopped. And Chirpy Cricket couldn't help feeling a bit disappointed, because he had hoped to enjoy a dance himself, to the Bumblebees' music when he left his home that evening.

A little later he told his favorite cousin about the party that had lasted all day. And Chirpy said that he supposed the Bumblebees had only one party

7

a year, because he understood that most of them were great workers, and he didn't believe they would care to spend a whole day humming, very often.

The favorite cousin gave Chirpy a strange look in the moonlight. And then he began to fiddle, making no remark whatsoever. He thought there was no use wasting words on a fine, warm night—just the sort of night for a lively cr-r-r-i! cr-r-r-i! cr-r-r-i!

Chirpy Cricket lost no time in getting his own fiddle to working. And each of them really believed he was himself making most of the music that was heard in the pasture.

Once in a while Chirpy Cricket and his cousin stopped to eat a little grass, or paused to carry a few spears into their holes, because they liked to have something to nibble on in the daytime. But they always returned to their fiddling again; and they never stopped for good until almost morning.

But at last Chirpy Cricket announced that he would make no more music that night.

"I'll go home now," he said. "I expect to have a good day's rest. And I'll meet you at this same spot to-morrow night for a little fiddling."

"I'll be here," his favorite cousin promised.

IV

TOO MUCH MUSIC

It was just beginning to grow light in the east when Chirpy Cricket crawled into his hole in the pasture, after his fiddling with his favorite cousin. Having spent a good deal of the previous day in listening to the humming of the musical Bumblebee family, who lived next door to him, Chirpy was more than ready to rest.

All was quiet at that hour of the morning, except for the creaky fiddling of a relation of Chirpy's who didn't appear to know that it was time to go home. But Chirpy Cricket didn't mind that. Fiddling never bothered him.

He never knew whether he had fallen asleep or not. He may have been only day-dreaming. Anyhow, all at once he noticed a rumbling sound, which grew louder and louder as he listened.

"They're at it again!" Chirpy Cricket exclaimed. "The Bumblebee family have begun their music. I do hope they aren't going to have another all-day party, for I don't want my rest disturbed."

But he soon found that the Bumblebees were not tuning up for nothing. Before long they were humming and buzzing away as if they hadn't a care in the world.

"I declare," — Chirpy cried, although there was no one but himself to hear — "I declare, they're dancing again! It can't be long after sunrise, either. And no doubt they won't stop till sunset."

He began to feel very much upset. He could understand why people should want to make music by night, and hop about in a lively fashion, too. But by day — ah! that was another matter.

Being unable to rest, on account of the uproar from the Bumblebees' house, Chirpy crept out of his door and stood blinking in the pasture. Soon he noticed a plump person sitting on a head of clover which the cows had overlooked. Chirpy couldn't see clearly who he was, coming up out of the

9

darkness as he had. But he was glad there was somebody to talk to, anyhow.

"Good morning!" he greeted the person on the clover-top, adding in a lower tone, "They're a queer family—those Bumblebees!"

To his great dismay, the person to whom he had spoken began to buzz. And leaping nearer him, in order to see him better, Chirpy Cricket discovered that he had been talking to Buster Bumblebee! Buster was a blundering, good-natured chap. And to Chirpy's relief, instead of getting angry he merely laughed.

"I didn't mean to hurt your feelings," Chirpy told him. "If I'm disagreeable this morning, it's because I need a good rest. And your family's humming disturbs me."

"Why do you think we're queer?" Buster asked him.

"Don't you call it a bit odd—having a dance at this time of day?"

"Bless you! They're not dancing in there!" Buster Bumblebee cried. "That's the workers storing away the honey. They're always buzzing like that. Perhaps you didn't know that our honey-makers can't work without being noisy. To tell the truth, they wake me every morning. And often I'd rather sleep."

"Will they keep this racket up all summer?" Chirpy inquired.

"On all pleasant days!" Buster Bumblebee said.

"Then," said Chirpy Cricket, "I'll have to move to a quieter neighborhood. This humming every day would soon drive me frantic."

"I don't blame you," Buster Bumblebee told him. "I've often felt that way myself."

V

A LIGHT IN THE DARK

Chirpy Cricket preferred the dark to the day. He was quite different from Jennie Junebug and Mehitable Moth, who dearly loved a light at night, and would dash joyously into any they saw.

There was only one light that Chirpy Cricket was always glad to see. He thought Freddie Firefly's flashes looked very cheerful as they twinkled about the farmyard. And he often told Freddie that he would be willing to linger above ground in the daytime now and then, if only Freddie would stay with him and make merry with his light.

But Freddie Firefly knew enough to decline the invitation. He was well aware that nobody could see his light when the sun was shining. And he was afraid that other merrymakers in the farmyard might make matters far from merry for him. For Freddie Firefly feared all birds. At night he used his trusty light to frighten Mr. Nighthawk or Willie Whip-poor-will. But he didn't intend to run any risk in the daytime, with Jolly Robin or Rusty Wren.

Chirpy Cricket soon saw that it was useless to try to get Freddie Firefly to enjoy an outing with him by daylight. So every night he spent as much time as he could in Freddie's company.

If the truth were known, Chirpy Cricket wished that he had a light of his own. And he couldn't help hoping that sooner or later Freddie Firefly would offer to lend him his.

Night after night the two met in the farmyard. But nothing seemed further from Freddie Firefly's thoughts than lending his brilliant greenish-white light to Chirpy Cricket, or to any one else.

But Chirpy simply couldn't keep his eyes off that wonderful flash-light when Freddie Firefly was in the neighborhood. People began to notice that he even stopped fiddling sometimes, to stare at Freddie Firefly.

11

At last Chirpy Cricket made up his mind that if he was ever going to borrow the light he would have to ask Freddie for it. Several nights passed before he could think of a good reason for using it. But after a while he thought of a fine one. So he went straight to Freddie Firefly.

"I'm going to see Miss Christabel Cricket home after the music is over tonight," Chirpy said, "and I've been wondering if you'd be willing to do me a favor."

"Why, certainly!" Freddie Firefly told him.

"Will you loan me your light?" Chirpy asked him. "You know there'll be no moon when it's time to go home. And your light would be a great help to me, for Miss Christabel lives beyond the barnyard fence."

For just a few moments Freddy Firefly appeared greatly surprised. To tell the truth, Chirpy's request almost took his breath away. And while he recovered himself he forgot to flash his light—a most unusual oversight.

But Freddie was no person to disappoint a friend. Besides, he had just said, "Why, certainly!"

Really, there was nothing for him to do but to say the same thing again.

VI

A PLAN GOES WRONG

Chirpy Cricket never fiddled faster than he did that night. Somehow he had a notion that the faster he fiddled the more quickly the night would pass. For Freddie Firefly had promised to loan Chirpy his light, because Chirpy needed it when he saw Miss Christabel Cricket to her home beyond the barnyard fence. Chirpy was going to see her safely to her door when the night's concert was ended. And he could hardly wait until the time came when he would flash that wonderful light in the eyes of all his friends.

"I hope you won't go dancing across the meadow tonight," he remarked anxiously to Freddie Firefly. "You might wander into the swamp and get lost."

"Oh, there's no danger of that!" Freddie assured him.

"If you stumbled into the wet swamp you might put your light out," Chirpy Cricket warned him.

But Freddie Firefly laughed and told him not to worry.

"I always enjoy at least one dance in the meadow each night," he explained. "They're expecting me over there now. And I don't want to disappoint them."

"No!" Chirpy answered. "And neither do you want to disappoint me. So please don't fail to be on hand when the music's finished."

After telling Chirpy that he wouldn't fail him, Freddie Firefly flitted away. But in spite of what he had said Chirpy Cricket couldn't help feeling nervous and uneasy. And he fiddled so fast that the other fiddlers kept complaining. They said he wasn't playing in time.

Chirpy Cricket was too well-mannered to contradict them. But he had his own opinion, which he kept to himself. He thought his companions were out of time. "Goodness!" he exclaimed under his breath. "I near heard such slow fiddling in all my life!"

There was another way, too, in which Chirpy annoyed the others. He kept asking them — first one and then another — what time it was. And of course nobody wants to stop and look at his watch when he is fiddling.

At last one of his cousins told him, in answer to his question, that it was time to stop talking and pay attention to the music.

After that Chirpy Cricket tried to be patient. But it was hard not to be restless. And he kept leaping into the air, hoping to get a glimpse of Freddie Firefly's twinkling light. For it seemed to him that Freddie would never return from the meadow.

At last the fiddlers stopped playing, one after another; for the night was going fast. The Cricket family always liked to be home before daylight.

Chirpy had almost given up hope of seeing Freddie Firefly. But to his great delight Freddie came skipping up just as Chirpy stood before Miss Christabel Cricket, whom he expected to see to her home.

"I'm glad you've come!" Chirpy greeted him. "I'll take your light now. And I'll return it to you to-morrow night."

"Oh! That would be too much trouble for you," Freddie Firefly said. "I'll go right along with you and your young lady. And after I've lighted her home I'll do the same thing for you."

"Oh! That would be too much trouble for you," Chirpy Cricket objected. "Let me take the light, please!" He certainly didn't want Freddie Firefly tagging along with Miss Christabel Cricket and himself.

Of course, Freddie Firefly couldn't give Chirpy his light. It was just as much a part of him as his head. And since Chirpy Cricket began to get excited, and said again and again that the light had been promised him, in the end Freddie had to explain everything.

It was a great disappointment to Chirpy Cricket. He had expected to have wonderful fun, flashing Freddie Firefly's light.

But Miss Christabel Cricket did not seem to mind in the least.

"You oughtn't to blame Freddie Firefly for not loaning his light," she said. "You know you wouldn't let him take your fiddle."

Well, Chirpy Cricket hadn't thought of that. And he had to admit that what she said was true.

And just then the sun peeped over Blue Mountain. So everybody hurried home alone, after all.

VII

JOHNNIE GREEN'S GUEST

There were enough night noises before Chirpy Cricket came to live in the farmyard. What with Solomon Owl's hooting, his cousin Simon Screecher's quavering call, and the musical Frog's family's concerts in Cedar Swamp, it was a wonder that Johnnie Green ever managed to fall asleep. The Katydids alone were almost enough to drive anybody frantic — if he let himself listen to them — with their everlasting cry of Katy did, Katy did; she did, she did.

Johnnie Green himself said he wished the Crickets had gone somewhere else to spend the summer. At least, he thought they might play some other tune besides cr-r-r-i! cr-r-r-i! cr-r-r-i! over and over again. If they would only fiddle "Yankee Doodle" now and then he said he wouldn't mind lying awake a while to listen to it.

Perhaps Chirpy Cricket heard what Johnnie Green said. Maybe he wanted to punish him. Anyhow, he crept into the farmhouse one evening and found his way into Johnnie Green's chamber, where he hid in a gaping crack behind the baseboard. And that very night, as soon as Johnnie Green put out his light and jumped into bed, Chirpy Cricket began to fiddle for him.

Johnnie had been sleepy. But the moment Chirpy Cricket began fiddling right there in his room he became wide awake. He had had no idea how loudly one of the Cricket family could play his cr-r-r-i! cr-r-r-i! cr-r-r-i! indoors. The high, shrill sound was piercing. It rang in Johnnie's ears and drowned the muffled concert of the fields and swamp which the light breeze bore through the window.

For a few minutes Johnnie lay still. And then he sat up in bed. "I'll have to get up and find that fellow," he said. "If I don't, he'll keep me awake."

The moment he stirred, the fiddling stopped short. Johnnie was glad of that. And once more he laid his head upon his pillow. But in a few moments that cr-r-r-i! cr-r-r-i! rang out again.

Then Johnnie Green tried several remedies. He shook the bed. He knocked over a chair. He caught up a shoe and threw it toward a corner of the room, whence the sound seemed to come. And then he threw the other shoe.

Every time Johnnie Green made a noise Chirpy Cricket stopped fiddling. And if Johnnie had had enough shoes no doubt he could have kept Chirpy from making any more music that night. But of course Johnnie couldn't have slept any, if he had done that. Besides, he would have kept the whole family awake, too. He thought of that after he had hurled the second shoe. For his father called up the stairs and asked him what was the matter.

"There's an old Cricket in my room!" Johnnie explained. "He's keeping me awake."

"I should think you were keeping him awake," said Farmer Green. "Get up and look for him if you must.... But don't let him bite you!"

"You wouldn't joke if this old Cricket was in your room," Johnnie grumbled.

He did not grumble often. But he had had a long, hard day, swimming in the mill-pond and climbing apple trees. And he wanted to go to sleep.

Johnnie Green thought it was no time to crack jokes.

VIII

PLEASING JOHNNIE GREEN

Johnnie Green knew that he could never find the Cricket in the dark. So he crawled out of bed and lighted a candle, blinking a few moments in its flickering flame.

From his hiding place in the crack of the baseboard, in a corner of Johnnie Green's chamber, Chirpy Cricket saw the gleam of the candle. And he wondered whether it might be a relation of Freddie Firefly. It seemed to have a trick of moving about in a jerky fashion, as if it didn't know where it was going and didn't greatly care, so long as it was on the move.

Chirpy Cricket kept still as a mouse then. He soon saw that the bearer of the bright light was quite unlike Freddie Firefly, in one way. He made a tremendous racket, knocking over almost everything in the room.

In a few minutes a voice called up the stairway again. "Is the Cricket chasing you?" it asked. It was Farmer Green, speaking to Johnnie.

"Don't tease me!" Johnnie Green cried. "Come up and help me find him!"

So Farmer Green climbed the stairs and looked into Johnnie's room and laughed.

"Maybe I ought to have brought the old shotgun," he said. "I'd hate to have a Cricket jump at me."

Johnnie managed to grin at that. He was so wide awake that he no longer felt like grumbling.

"The trouble with this Cricket is that he won't jump," he told his father. "I can't tell where he is, because he keeps still whenever I move. But when the light's out and everything's quiet he makes a terrible noise."

"That's a trick Crickets have," Farmer Green observed. "And I must say that if I were a Cricket I'd act the same way."

Of course Chirpy Cricket heard everything that was said. And he couldn't help thinking that Farmer Green was a very sensible person. "I dare say he'd be a famous fiddler if he belonged to our family," Chirpy told himself. And for a moment or two he was tempted to play a tune for Farmer Green. But he thought better of the notion at once. He remembered that Farmer Green had climbed the stairs to hunt for him. And Chirpy squeezed himself further into the crack where he was hiding until he was so huddled up that he couldn't have fiddled if he had wanted to.

Though they looked carefully, neither Johnnie nor his father could find him. And at last they had to admit that it was useless to search any longer.

"What shall I do?" Johnnie wailed. "As soon as I put out the light and get into bed he'll begin chirping again."

"In such cases," Farmer Green answered wisely, "there's only one thing to do."

"What's that?" Johnnie inquired hopefully.

"All you can do," said Farmer Green, "is to come downstairs and have something to eat."

Now, that may seem a strange remedy. But somehow it just suited Johnnie Green. He pattered barefooted down the stairs. And later, when he went to bed again, and Chirpy Cricket began to chirp once more, all Johnnie Green said was this:

"Sing away — little Tommy Tucker! You may not know it, but you sang for my supper!"

And the next moment, Johnnie Green was sound asleep.

IX

AN INTERRUPTED NAP

Chirpy Cricket liked his home in Farmer Green's yard. During the long summer days he thought it very cheerful to rest in his dark hole in the ground. He liked the darkness of his home; he liked its warmth, too. For in pleasant weather the sun beat down upon the straw-littered ground above him and gave him plenty of heat, while on gray days the straw blanket kept his house cosy. And it never occurred to Chirpy Cricket that there was anything odd in having a blanket over his house instead of over himself.

Nothing ever really disturbed Chirpy Cricket after he settled in the farmyard. To be sure, he had a few frights at first. Now and then the earth trembled in a terrible fashion. But that happened only when Johnnie Green led old Ebenezer, or some other horse, to the watering-trough, passing right over Chirpy's home. And Chirpy had soon learned that he was in no danger.

Then at other times he heard an odd tearing and scratching, as if some giant had discovered Chirpy's doorway and meant to dig him out of his hiding place. By peeping slyly out he discovered at last the cause of those fearful sounds. It was only the hens looking for something to eat—a bit of grain amid the straw, or perhaps an angleworm. Chirpy never left his house when he heard the hens at work. He had no wish to offer himself as a tidbit. And he felt quite safe down in his home, for he was quick to learn that the hens were no diggers. They could only scratch the surface of the ground. So, in time, he used to laugh when he heard them. And now and then he would even fiddle a bit, as if to say to them, "Here I am! Come and get me if you can!"

The sound of fiddling, coming from beneath their feet, always puzzled the hens. They would stop scratching and cock their heads on one side, to listen. And they tried to look very knowing. But they were really the most stupid of all the creatures in the farmyard. If they had only been as wise as Farmer Green's cat they would have kept still and waited and watched.

And sooner or later they would have given Chirpy Cricket the surprise of his life, when he came crawling out of his hole to get a few blades of grass for his supper.

But even if the hens had thought of such a plan they never could have kept their minds upon it long enough to carry it out. So perhaps it was no wonder that Chirpy Cricket got the idea into his head that he was safe from everybody. Sometimes, when he was dozing, even the footsteps of old Ebenezer failed to rouse him.

But there came a day when Chirpy Cricket awoke with a great start. Something had touched his long feelers. Something had come right down into his hole and was prodding him.

He thought it must be a hen. And he did not laugh. No! Nor did he fiddle!

X

CAUGHT!

Whatever or whoever it was that had entered Chirpy Cricket's home—the hole in the ground near Farmer Green's barn—it caused him a terrible fright. It kept poking him in a most alarming fashion. Chirpy couldn't move away from it, for his home was only big enough for himself alone. And since he didn't care to share it with another, he soon made up his mind that there was only one thing for him to do. He would quit his house for the time being, with the hope of finding it empty later. Indeed Chirpy Cricket thought he would be lucky to escape in safety. So he scrambled up into the daylight, to be greeted with a shout and a pounce, both at the same time. And Chirpy Cricket saw, too late, that it was a creature much bigger than a hen that had captured him. It was Johnnie Green!

Of course Johnnie himself had not entered Chirpy's underground home. What he had done was merely to run a straw into the hole where Chirpy lived and prod him with it until he came out.

"Aha!" said Johnnie Green as he looked at his prisoner, whom he held gingerly between a finger and a thumb. "Are you the rascal that keeps me awake at night with your everlasting noise?"

Chirpy Cricket never said a word.

"You make racket enough every night," Johnnie told him. "Can't you answer now when you're spoken to?"

Still Chirpy Cricket made no reply. He waved his feelers frantically and tried to jump out of Johnnie Green's grasp. But no matter how fast he moved his six legs, he couldn't get away.

"You don't seem to like me," said his captor finally. "You don't act as if you wanted to play with me.... What will you do for me if I let you go?"

But not a word did Chirpy Cricket say—not one single word!

22

"You're a queer one," Johnnie Green told him. "You might fiddle for me, at least—though I must say I don't care for the tune you always play. I can get better music out of a cornstalk fiddle than I've ever heard from you or any of your family."

Then, very carefully, Johnnie set Chirpy Cricket on the ground, with both his hands cupped closely over him, so he couldn't jump away.

"Now, fiddle!" Johnnie Green cried. "Fiddle just once and I'll let you go."

Though Johnnie Green waited patiently for what seemed to him a long time, he heard nothing that sounded the least bit like fiddling. So at last he peeped between two fingers to see what the fiddler was doing. But Johnnie Green couldn't see him. Little by little he lifted his hands. And to his great surprise there was nothing under them but grass—and beneath the grass a crack in the earth.

"Well! You're a sly one!" Johnnie Green exclaimed. "You've crawled into that crack. And you may stay there, too, for all I care." Johnnie jumped to his feet and moved away. And not until he had been gone some time did Chirpy Cricket make a sound. Then he played a few notes on his fiddle, just to see that it hadn't been harmed.

XI

A QUEER, NEW COUSIN

Chirpy Cricket was so fond of fiddling that sometimes he was the last of all the big Cricket family to stop making music and go home to bed. Now and then he lingered so long above the ground that the dawn caught him before he crept into his hole in the ground, beneath the straw. And one morning it was getting so light before he had played enough to suit him that he crawled into a crack in Farmer Green's garden. It looked like a comfortable place to spend the day. And he thought it would be foolish for him to do much travelling at that hour, because there was no telling when an early bird might spy — and pounce upon — him.

He found his retreat quite to his liking. Nothing had happened to disturb his rest. And if he had only had time to carry a few blades of grass into the crack, to eat between naps, Chirpy would have had nothing to wish for.

Late in the afternoon, however, a most unusual thing took place. Chirpy Cricket noticed a sound as of some one digging. It grew louder and louder as he listened. And it was not in the least like the scratching of a hen, looking for grubs and worms. This noise was deep down in the ground and like nothing Chirpy had ever heard.

He wished that he had not allowed himself to become so fond of fiddling. If he had cared less for it, he would have gone home in good season. But there he was in a crack in the garden! And he didn't dare leave it because he had heard that the garden was a famous place for birds.

Chirpy Cricket was frightened. And when at last the loose earth near him began to quiver and even to crumble he was so scared that he didn't know which way to move. The next instant a strange looking person stood before him. And for a few moments neither one of them said a word.

The newcomer was a big fellow, very long and with enormous legs. His front legs especially were short and powerful, with huge feet at the end of

24

them. And yet, odd as the stranger was, Chirpy could not help noticing that somehow he had a look like the Cricket family.

"Well," said the stranger at last, "you seem surprised. Perhaps you weren't expecting callers."

"No, I wasn't," Chirpy Cricket answered in a voice that was faint from the fright he had had.

"But you're glad to see me, I hope," the stranger went on. "You know I'm related to you. You know I'm a sort of cousin of yours."

"Is that so?" Chirpy Cricket cried. "I did think for a moment that there was a slight family resemblance. But the longer I look at you the queerer you seem. May I ask your name?"

"I'm Mr. Mole Cricket," said the stranger. "And I don't need to inquire who you are. You're one of the well-known Field Cricket family."

XII

AN UNDERGROUND CHAT

Chirpy Cricket was glad of one thing. Mr. Mole Cricket talked quite pleasantly, for all he looked so frightful. When he dug his way through the dirt in Farmer Green's garden and broke into the crack where Chirpy was hiding he had given Chirpy a terrible start.

"If you're a cousin of mine—as you say—it's strange that I've never happened to meet you before," Chirpy told the newcomer.

"Not at all! Not at all!" Mr. Mole Cricket said. "I spend all my time underground. I've never been up in the open."

"Don't you go out at night?" Chirpy asked him.

"Never!" Mr. Mole Cricket declared. "I've lived my whole life in the dirt. And I like it too well to leave it."

Chirpy Cricket thought his cousin was the queerest person he had ever met.

"How do you get anything to eat?" he inquired.

Mr. Mole Cricket seemed to consider that an odd question.

"Bless you!" he exclaimed. "There's everything to eat in the ground— everything anybody could possibly want. Wherever I tunnel I find tender roots. You know Farmer Green grows fine vegetables here. Indeed that's one reason I live under his garden."

"If that's one reason, what's another?" Chirpy Cricket asked him. For Chirpy couldn't help being curious about this new-found cousin of his, who had such strange ways and who was even stranger to look upon.

He was obliging enough—was Mr. Mole Cricket. He was quite willing to answer any and all questions. It may be that he was glad of the chance to talk with somebody. Certainly it seemed to Chirpy Cricket that his cousin led a very lonely life. He explained to Chirpy that it was easy to dig in the garden, because its soil was loose. The ploughing in the spring, and the harrowing, as well as the hoeing that Farmer Green's hired man did during the summer, kept the earth in fine condition for tunnelling. Of course, living beneath the surface as he did, Mr. Mole Cricket had no way of knowing why the garden soil was so nicely stirred up. He only knew that it was so. And that was quite enough for him.

Chirpy Cricket said that it was all very interesting to hear about. But he knew that he shouldn't care to follow Mr. Mole Cricket's manner of living. "I love to fiddle," he said. "I simply must go abroad every pleasant night and make music."

"But you don't need to leave the dirt to fiddle!" Mr. Mole Cricket exclaimed. "I'm musical too. I often fiddle down in my house. I don't know a better way of passing the time, when a person's not digging or eating."

"Won't you play for me now?" Chirpy Cricket asked him.

Mr. Mole Cricket was more than willing to oblige. He began to fiddle at once. And the tune he played was as strange as he was. Chirpy Cricket did not like it at all. It seemed to him very mournful, a sort of sad, sad air, as if Mr. Mole Cricket were bewailing his dismal life beneath the garden.

But of course Chirpy was too polite to tell that to his cousin. And when Mr. Mole Cricket asked him how he liked the tune, Chirpy replied that it was very, very interesting.

XIII

A QUESTION OF FEET

"Are you sure you're a cousin of mine?" Chirpy Cricket inquired of Mr. Mole Cricket. "Don't you think that perhaps you are mistaken? I'm almost certain you are."

"No!" said Mr. Mole Cricket. "I can't be wrong. Why do you ask me such a question?"

"Your forefeet"—Chirpy told him—"your forefeet are so big! I've always understood that all our family had small ones."

Mr. Mole Cricket smiled.

"Don't let the size of my feet trouble you!" he replied. "I couldn't be a Mole Cricket if my feet were like yours. You see, I use my forefeet for digging. And if they weren't big and strong I never could burrow in this garden, nor anywhere else."

Still Chirpy Cricket had his doubts.

"I'm inclined to believe," he continued, "that you're related to Grandfather Mole, and not to me. For your feet are very much like his."

"Oh, no!" Mr. Mole Cricket cried. "And for pity's sake don't ever let Grandfather Mole hear you say that! He'd be so angry that he'd eat me, as likely as not. You see, he objects to my name. He says I have no right to call myself Mr. Mole Cricket. But that's the name my family has always had. And I can't very well change it."

The poor fellow acted so alarmed that Chirpy Cricket hastened to promise him that he would never mention his likeness to Grandfather Mole again.

"Very well!" said Mr. Mole Cricket. "That's kind of you, I'm sure. And now, if you want to make me quite happy, there's one more thing to which you will agree."

"What's that?" Chirpy Cricket asked. He felt sorry for Mr. Mole Cricket, who had never known the pleasure of fiddling with a thousand other musicians under the stars on a warm summer night. "If there is anything I can do to make you happy, just tell me!"

"Then call me 'Cousin'!" Mr. Mole Cricket begged him.

Chirpy Cricket cast one glance at Mr. Mole Cricket's huge feet. In spite of everything their owner had told him, Chirpy still found it difficult to believe that Mr. Mole Cricket could be even a very distant relation.

"I'll do it!" he said at last. "If it will make you any happier I'll call you 'Cousin' — though you can't be any nearer than a hundred times removed."

It was easy to see that Mr. Mole Cricket was delighted.

"Thank you! Thank you!" he exclaimed. "But permit me to correct you. I'm your cousin a good many thousand times removed. But that's no reason why we shouldn't be the best of friends. And now," he added, "won't you come home with me? I'd like you to meet my wife."

While thanking him for the invitation, Chirpy Cricket couldn't help wondering whether Mr. Mole Cricket's wife had as big feet as her husband.

XIV

CHIRPY IS CAREFUL

"Do you live near-by?" Chirpy Cricket inquired of Mr. Mole Cricket, who had just invited him to his home to meet his wife.

"My home is not very far from here," his new cousin said. "We'll go back through this tunnel I've been making. The other end of it opens into my dwelling, some distance below the surface of the garden. Follow me and you'll have no trouble finding it."

But somehow Chirpy Cricket did not quite like the idea of travelling with the stranger, cousin though he might be, under Farmer Green's garden. "Not to-day!" he said politely. "I haven't had anything to eat since last night. And I don't feel like taking a journey."

"We'll snatch a bite on the way to my house," Mr. Mole Cricket suggested cheerfully. "I'll dig out a few juicy roots for you. Which kind do you like best—beet, turnip or carrot?"

"I don't like any of them," Chirpy Cricket confessed.

"You don't!" his cousin cried, as if he were astonished to hear that. "What do you live on, then?"

"Grass!" Chirpy answered.

"I've never heard of it," said Mr. Mole Cricket. "And I must say you have queer tastes—even though you are my own cousin."

Chirpy Cricket saw that he and Mr. Mole Cricket were bound to have trouble if they saw too much of each other. So he hinted—in a delicate way—that Mr. Mole Cricket's wife must be wondering where he was.

Thereupon that gentleman started up hurriedly and made for his tunnel.

"I'll see you again sometime," he said hastily over his shoulder. And in another instant he was gone.

They never met again. Chirpy Cricket took great pains never to spend another day in hiding in Farmer Green's garden. He was afraid there might be trouble if he saw more of his cousin. And he couldn't forget those powerful forelegs and enormous feet of Mr. Mole Cricket! They looked very dangerous.

The longer Chirpy pondered over his brief meeting with Mr. Mole Cricket, the more firmly he made up his mind that he had been in great danger and that he had been lucky to escape alive. Everybody knew that Grandfather Mole was a terrible-tempered person when aroused. He would rush at anybody, big or little. Perhaps that was because he couldn't see what sized person he was attacking. For Grandfather Mole was blind. But he never stopped to inquire of anybody whether he was tall or short, thick or thin. He just went ahead without asking.

"I'm glad," thought Chirpy, "that I didn't go home with Mr. Mole Cricket. If his wife's feet are anything like his they'd be a fearful pair to quarrel with. And even if they hadn't quarrelled with me, they might have had trouble between themselves. And if I happened to get in their way it would certainly have gone hard with me."

Harmless Mr. Mole Cricket never knew what a monster his cousin Chirpy Cricket believed him to be. When he reached home he told his wife that he had met a queer little cousin who spent much of his time above ground and lived on grass.

But Mrs. Mole Cricket wouldn't believe him. She told him not to be silly. She even said that there wasn't any such thing as grass. And she asked him how anybody could live on it when there wasn't any anywhere.

Naturally, she wouldn't have talked like that if she had ever seen much of the world. But she had spent her whole life down in the dirt, beneath Farmer Green's garden.

TOMMY TREE CRICKET

After meeting that odd Mr. Mole Cricket, who claimed to be his cousin, Chirpy Cricket tried to find out more about him from his nearer relations. But there wasn't one that had ever seen or heard of such a person. One night Chirpy even travelled quite a distance to call on Tommy Tree Cricket, with the hope that perhaps Tommy might be able to tell him something.

Chirpy found Tommy Tree Cricket in the tangle of raspberry bushes beyond the garden. It was not hard to tell where he was, because he was a famous fiddler. He played a tune that was different from Chirpy's cr-r-r-i! cr-r-r-i! cr-r-r-i! Tommy Tree Cricket fiddled re-teat! re-teat! re-teat!And many considered him a much finer musician than Chirpy himself. He was small and pale. Beside Chirpy Cricket, who was all but black, Tommy Tree Cricket looked decidedly delicate. But he could fiddle all night without getting tired.

"I've come all the way from the yard to have a chat with you!" Chirpy called to his cousin Tommy.

"Come up and have a seat!" said Tommy Tree Cricket.

"I can find one here, thank you!" Chirpy answered.

"Oh! Don't sit on the damp ground!" Tommy cried. "That's a dangerous thing to do."

Chirpy Cricket smiled to himself. In a way Tommy Tree Cricket was queer. He always clung to trees and shrubs, claiming that it was much more healthful to live off the ground. But he was so pale that Chirpy Cricket was sure he was mistaken.

"The ground's good enough for me," Chirpy told his cousin.

"Well, we won't quarrel about that tonight," said Tommy Tree Cricket. "Sit there, if you will. And when I've finished playing this tune we'll have a talk. I only hope you won't catch cold while you're waiting down there."

"Can't you stop fiddling long enough to talk with me now?" Chirpy asked him. "I've come here to ask you whether you ever saw a cousin of ours called Mr. Mole Cricket."

"Re-teat! re-teat! re-teat!" Tommy Tree Cricket was already fiddling away as if it were the last night of the summer. He was making so much shrill music that he couldn't hear a word Chirpy said. The more Chirpy tried to attract his attention the harder he played, rolling his eyes in every direction—except that of his caller.

Several times Chirpy Cricket leaped into the air, hoping that Tommy Tree Cricket would see that he had something important to say. But Tommy paid not the slightest heed to him.

At last Chirpy decided that he might as well do a little fiddling himself, to pass the time away. So he began his cr-r-r-i! cr-r-r-i! cr-r-r-i! And then Tommy noticed him immediately.

"You're playing the wrong tune!" he cried. "It's re-teat! re-teat! re-teat!"

Chirpy Cricket thought that his cousin's face was slightly darker, as if a flush of annoyance had come over it. He certainly didn't want to quarrel with Tommy Tree Cricket. So he said to him, very mildly, "I fear you do not like my playing."

"I can't say that I do," said Tommy. "It makes me think of that creaking pump at the farmhouse."

"And of what"—Chirpy Cricket stammered—"of what, pray, does your own fiddling remind you?"

"Ah!" said Tommy. "My own music is like nothing in the world except the sound of a shimmering moonbeam."

There is no doubt that Tommy Tree Cricket thought very well of his own fiddling.

XVI

A LONG WAIT

Chirpy cricket was so good-natured that he wouldn't quarrel with his cousin, Tommy Tree Cricket. Although Tommy had said bluntly that Chirpy's fiddling reminded him of Farmer Green's creaking pump, Chirpy made no disagreeable answer. He did not want to hurt his pale cousin's feelings.

After making his rude remark Tommy Tree Cricket began his re-teat! re-teat! re-teat! once more. He shuffled his wings together at a faster rate than ever, as if he had to furnish all the music for the night. As before, he seemed to have forgotten all about his caller; for Chirpy still waited beneath the raspberry bush where Tommy Tree Cricket was fiddling.

But if Tommy paid no heed to Chirpy, there was a reason why. Near Tommy sat a pale young miss of his own sort, who listened with great enjoyment to his playing. Or at least she acted as if she thought it the most beautiful music in the whole world.

Tommy Tree Cricket was not so intent upon his fiddling that he couldn't roll his eyes towards his fair listener. And Chirpy was not slow to understand that it was for her that Tommy was playing his re-teat! re-teat! re-teat!

"I'll wait here until he rests," Chirpy said to himself. "Then I'll ask him again what he knows about Mr. Mole Cricket."

Well, Chirpy waited and waited. But it seemed to him that as the night lengthened Tommy Tree Cricket fiddled all the faster. And if the weather hadn't turned colder along toward morning probably he wouldn't have had a chance to speak to Tommy again.

Anyhow, a cool wind began to whip around the side of Blue Mountain and sweep through Pleasant Valley. And the moment it struck Tommy Tree Cricket he began to play more slowly. Little by little a longer pause crept between his re-teats. And at last the pale miss beside him cried, "I hope you're not going to stop your beautiful fiddling!"

"I fear I'll have to," Tommy told her with a sigh. "I'm beginning to feel a bit stiff, with this north wind blowing on me."

This was Chirpy Cricket's chance.

"Please!" he called. "Will you listen to me a moment?"

"What! Have you come back again?" Tommy Tree Cricket sang out.

"No! I've been here all the time," Chirpy explained. "I've been waiting for hours to have a talk with you."

"Very well!" Tommy answered. "It's too cold for me to fiddle any more. So talk away! And you'd better be quick about it, for the night's almost gone."

But somehow Chirpy Cricket felt that his chat could wait a little longer. If the pale young person clinging to the raspberry bush near Tommy Tree Cricket loved music, he thought it was a pity to disappoint her.

"You may feel too cold to fiddle; but I don't!" Chirpy said. "I'm quite warm down here on the ground. This little hollow where I'm sitting is sheltered from the wind. So I'll fiddle for your friend." As he spoke he began to play.

Looks as of great pain came over the pale faces of his two listeners in the raspberry bush. And they shuddered so violently that they had to cling tightly to their seats to keep from falling.

"My friend thanks you. But she says she doesn't care for your fiddling," Tommy Tree Cricket called down to Chirpy. "She says it's too squeaky."

Chirpy Cricket was fiddling so hard by that time that he never heard a word. And when he stopped at last, to rest a bit, a voice cried out, "That's fine! Won't you play some more?"

Chirpy Cricket was pleased. He thought, of course, that it was Tommy's friend speaking to him. But when he looked up he couldn't see her anywhere — nor her companion either.

They had both disappeared. And it was already gray in the east.

SITTING ON A LILY-PAD

Though Chirpy Cricket looked all around with great care, he couldn't discover who had spoken to him. A voice from somewhere had called out that his music was fine and asked him if he wouldn't play some more.

Whoever the owner of the voice might be, it was plain that he liked music. So without knowing for whom he was playing, Chirpy began to fiddle again. And when he stopped the same voice cried, "Thank you very much!"

Now, the duck-pond was near-by. And at first Chirpy hadn't thought of looking there for his listener. But the second time he heard the voice he guessed that it came from the pond. So Chirpy leaped to the water's edge; and there, sitting on a lily-pad, was the tiniest Frog he had ever seen. He seemed no bigger than Chirpy himself.

"How do you do!" Chirpy said to him. "Was it you that spoke to me?"

"Yes!" the stranger said. "I've been enjoying your music. And I'm glad to meet you. It's time we knew each other, living as we do in the same neighborhood. My name is Mr. Cricket Frog. And may I inquire what yours is?"

"I'm called Chirpy Cricket," said the fiddler on the bank. "Is it possible — do you think — that we are cousins?"

"No!" said Mr. Cricket Frog. "No! I belong to a branch of the well-known Tree Frog family. But somehow I've never cared to live in trees. Indeed, I've never climbed a tree in all my life."

"You're a sensible person!" Chirpy Cricket cried. He did not know that the reason why Mr. Cricket Frog stayed on the ground was because his feet were not suited to climbing trees. He couldn't have got up a tree if he had tried. "Aren't you afraid of falling off that lily-pad into the water?" Chirpy asked his new friend. "It seems to me you haven't picked out a safe place at all."

He had scarcely finished speaking when he had a great fright. For Mr. Cricket Frog did not answer him. Instead he leaped suddenly into the air. And Chirpy Cricket feared that he would fall into the water and be drowned. But when Mr. Cricket Frog came down again he landed squarely upon another lily-pad.

"I caught him," he said pleasantly.

Chirpy Cricket had no idea what he was talking about.

"Whom did you catch?" he asked.

"The fly!" Mr. Cricket Frog replied.

"Don't you think you took a great risk, leaping above the water like that?" Chirpy inquired. "Aren't you worried for fear you'll fall into the pond some day, if you jump for flies in that careless fashion?"

Mr. Cricket Frog tried not to smile.

"Bless you!" he exclaimed. "I spend half my time in the water. Please don't think I'm boasting when I say I'm a fine swimmer. You'll understand why when you look at my feet." And he held up a foot so that Chirpy Cricket might see it.

Chirpy noticed that there were webs between Mr. Cricket Frog's toes. And everybody knows that webbed feet are the best for swimming.

Mr. Cricket Frog wanted to be agreeable. "Would you like to see me swim?" he asked.

"Yes, thank you!" Chirpy replied.

So Mr. Cricket Frog leaped nimbly into the water and began to swim among the lily-pads while Chirpy watched him and admired his skill.

All at once Chirpy heard a splash. And he was just about to ask Mr. Cricket Frog what it could be, when he noticed something queer about his new friend. He was no longer swimming. He was floating, motionless, upon the water. Not by a single movement of any kind did he show that he was alive.

XVIII

MR. CRICKET FROG'S TRICK

"What's the matter? Are you hurt?" Chirpy Cricket called to Mr. Cricket Frog from the bank of the duck-pond. Ever since a splash near-by had interrupted their talk, Mr. Cricket Frog had not swum a single stroke. He was floating, motionless, upon the surface of the water. And he made no reply whatever to Chirpy's questions. He acted exactly as if he had not heard them. The fitful breeze caught at Mr. Cricket Frog's limp form and wafted it about.

Chirpy Cricket couldn't help being alarmed. And yet he almost thought, for a moment, that he saw Mr. Cricket Frog's eyes rolling in his direction, as he stood on the bank of the pond. If Mr. Cricket Frog was in trouble, Chirpy knew of no way to help him. And after a time he made up his mind that Mr. Cricket Frog was beyond anybody's help. Chirpy was about to go back to the farmyard when Mr. Cricket Frog came suddenly to life.

"Meet me here to-morrow!" he called. Then he dived to the bottom of the water. And Chirpy Cricket went home, thinking that it was all very queer.

"What happened to you yesterday?" Chirpy asked Mr. Cricket Frog, when he came back to the duck-pond the following day and found that spry little gentleman waiting for him on a lily-pad. "Were you ill?"

"Oh, no!" Mr. Cricket Frog answered. "When I heard a splash behind me I didn't know who made it. So I played dead for a while. And after waiting until I felt somewhat safer, I went down to the bottom of the pond and hid in the mud. I've found that it's always wise to attract as little attention as possible when I don't know who's lurking about.... I hope you didn't think I was rude," he added.

"No!" Chirpy told him. "But I've been upset ever since I saw you. I haven't had the heart to fiddle."

"Dear me!" Mr. Cricket Frog cried. "I must do something to cheer you up. I'll sing you a song!" Then Mr. Cricket Frog puffed out his yellow throat and began to sing. And he gave Chirpy Cricket a great surprise. For his singing was so like Chirpy's fiddling that Chirpy thought for a moment he was making the sound himself.

But there was one marked difference. Mr. Cricket Frog's time was not like his. It was not regular. Mr. Cricket Frog began to sing somewhat slowly and gradually sang faster and faster. After he had sung about thirty notes he would pause to get his breath. And then he would begin again, exactly as before.

Mr. Cricket Frog hadn't sung long before Chirpy's spirits began to rise. Indeed, he soon felt so cheerful that he began to fiddle. And between the two they made such a chirping that an old drake swam across the duck-pond to see what was going on.

Of course, his curiosity put an end to the concert. Mr. Cricket Frog saw him coming. And this time he didn't stop to play dead. He sank in a great hurry to the bottom of the pond.

Chirpy Cricket wondered why his friend chose to stay in a place where there were so many interruptions. "I should think," he said to himself, "Mr. Cricket Frog would rather live in a hole in the ground, as I do.... I must ask him, when I see him again, why he doesn't move to the farmyard."

Mr. Cricket Frog was very polite, later, when Chirpy spoke to him about moving. But he explained that he was too fond of swimming to do that. And besides, he thought his voice sounded better on water than it did on land.

XIX

IT WASN'T THUNDER

Quite often, during the nightly concerts in which Chirpy Cricket took part, he had noticed an odd cry, Peent! Peent! which seemed to come from the woods. And sometimes there followed from the same direction a hollow, booming sound, as if somebody were amusing himself by blowing across the bung-hole of an empty barrel.

Chirpy Cricket had a great curiosity to know who made those queer noises. He asked everybody he met about them. And at last Kiddie Katydid told him that it was Mr. Nighthawk that he had heard.

"He seems to think he's a musician," said Chirpy Cricket. "But I must say I don't care much for his music. He's not what you might call a steady player. And his notes are not shrill enough for my liking. Perhaps he lacks training. I'd be glad to take him in hand and see what I could do with him. Tell me! Does he ever visit our neighborhood?"

"Not often!" said Kiddie Katydid. "I met him here once. And that was enough for me. I never felt more uncomfortable in all my life." He shuddered as he spoke and looked over his shoulder.

Somehow Chirpy Cricket did not share Kiddie Katydid's uneasiness. The more he thought about Mr. Nighthawk the more he wanted to meet him.

"If you ever see Mr. Nighthawk again I wish you'd tell him I want to talk with him," Chirpy said.

"I'll do so," Kiddie Katydid promised. "And now let me give you a bit of advice. When you meet Mr. Nighthawk, keep perfectly still. He's a hungry fellow, always on the look-out for somebody to eat. But he has one peculiar habit: he won't grab you unless you're moving through the air. He always takes his food on the wing."

Chirpy thanked his friend Kiddie Katydid for this valuable bit of news. And he said he'd be sure to remember it.

"Well," Kiddie Katydid observed, "if you forget it when you meet Mr. Nighthawk you'll forget it only once. For he'll grab you quick as a flash."

Chirpy Cricket pondered a good deal over the talk he had with Kiddie Katydid. It was clear that Mr. Nighthawk was a dangerous person. "Perhaps" — Chirpy thought — "perhaps if I could get him to take a greater interest in his music he wouldn't be so ferocious. Yes! I feel sure that if I could only persuade him to practice that booming sound it would give Mr. Nighthawk something pleasant to think of. Who knows but that he might become as gentle as I am?"

Chirpy Cricket liked that notion so much that he thought of little else. He even began to consider making a journey to the woods where Mr. Nighthawk lived, in order to meet that gentleman and offer to train him to be a better musician. And at last Chirpy had even decided to go — as soon as the moon should be full. He spent much of his time listening for Mr. Nighthawk's Peent! Peent! which now and then came faintly across the meadow, and the dull, muffled boom that often followed.

While Chirpy waited for the moon to grow full, one night an odd thing happened. The stars twinkled overhead. There wasn't a cloud in the sky. Yet all at once a loud boom startled Chirpy Cricket and made him leap suddenly towards home.

"Goodness!" he cried to Kiddie Katydid, who happened to be near him. "Did you hear the thunder?"

"That wasn't thunder," Kiddie said. "And you'd better not jump like that again. Mr. Nighthawk is here. He made that sound himself."

XX

BOUND TO BE DIFFERENT

Nothing ever surprised Chirpy Cricket more than what Kiddie Katydid told him. He had thought it was thunder that he had just heard. But it was Mr. Nighthawk, making that odd, booming sound of his. It was ever so much louder than Chirpy had supposed it could be. He had never heard it so near before.

For a moment Chirpy thought that perhaps Kiddie Katydid didn't know what he was talking about. But no! There was Mr. Nighthawk's well-known call, Peent! Peent! There was no denying that it was his voice. He always talked through his nose—or so it sounded. And one couldn't mistake it.

Chirpy Cricket began to think that after all he would rather not have a talk with Mr. Nighthawk. He certainly sounded terrible!

Meanwhile Mr. Nighthawk alighted in a tree right over Chirpy's head, and settled himself lengthwise along a limb. He was, indeed, an odd person. He liked to be different from other folk. And just because other birds sat crosswise on a perch, Mr. Nighthawk had to sit in exactly the opposite fashion. No doubt if he could have, he would have hung underneath the limb by his heels, like Benjamin Bat. Only he would have wanted to hang by his nose instead of his heels, in order to be different.

"Has anybody seen Chirpy Cricket?" Mr. Nighthawk sang out.

"He's on the ground, under that tree you're in," Kiddie Katydid informed him. Kiddie never moved as he spoke, but clung closely to a twig in the bush where he was hiding. Being green himself, he hardly thought that Mr. Nighthawk would be able to discover him amongst shrubbery of the same color.

Chirpy Cricket wished that Kiddie Katydid hadn't replied to Mr. Nighthawk at all. But how could Kiddie know that Chirpy had changed his mind? And now Mr. Nighthawk spoke to Chirpy.

"I can't see you very well, Mr. Cricket," he said. "Won't you leap into the air a few times, so I can get a good look at you? I've heard that you've been wanting to meet me. And I've come all the way from the woods just to please you."

Luckily Chirpy Cricket did not forget Kiddie Katydid's advice. Kiddie had explained to him how Mr. Nighthawk caught his meals on the wing.

"You'll have to excuse me," Chirpy told Mr. Nighthawk. "I'd rather not do any jumping for you. That wasn't why I wanted to meet you."

"Ha!" said Mr. Nighthawk. "Then why — pray — did you wish to see me?"

"I thought" — Chirpy Cricket replied — "I thought that perhaps you'd like me to help you with your music. I've often heard your booming at a distance. And it has seemed to me that you have the making of a good musician, if you have a good teacher."

Mr. Nighthawk sniffed. It must be remembered that he was not very gentlemanly.

"I've had plenty of training," he said. "I didn't come all the way from the woods to be told that I don't know my own business. I practice every night. And I flatter myself that I'm a perfect performer."

"Then," said Chirpy Cricket, "perhaps you need a new fiddle. For there's no doubt that your booming would sound much better if it were shriller."

Mr. Nighthawk gave a rude laugh.

"I don't make that sound with a fiddle," he sneered. "Don't you know a wind instrument when you hear it?"

MR. NIGHTHAWK EXPLAINS

Mr. Nighthawk appeared to think it a great joke on Chirpy Cricket, because Chirpy had thought he played the fiddle. He laughed in a most disagreeable fashion. And he kept repeating that people who didn't know a wind instrument when they heard it couldn't know much about music.

As for Chirpy, he didn't know just what to say. But at last he managed to stammer that he hoped he hadn't offended Mr. Nighthawk.

"Not at all!" Mr. Nighthawk told him. "This is the funniest thing I've heard for a long time. It was worth coming all the way from the woods to enjoy a laugh over it."

Of course it was very rude for Mr. Nighthawk to speak in such a way. But he was never polite to any of the smaller field-people, unless he happened to be coaxing them to jump, so that he might grab them when they were in the air. You may be sure he was as meek as he could be if he happened to meet Solomon Owl. But at that moment Solomon was far off in the hemlock woods. Only a short time before Mr. Nighthawk had heard his rolling call in the distance. So he felt quite safe in bullying so gentle a creature as Chirpy Cricket.

Thinking that he ought to be polite to his caller, rude as he was, Chirpy asked Mr. Nighthawk if he wouldn't kindly play something.

"I don't care if I do," said Mr. Nighthawk—meaning that he did care, and that he would play something. But it was not because he wanted to oblige anybody. He was proud of his booming. And he was only too glad of a chance to show Chirpy Cricket how loud he could make it sound.

"Stay right there in that tree, if you will!" Chirpy said. "I won't move. I'll sit here and listen."

"Ha, ha!" Mr. Nighthawk laughed. "I knew you didn't know anything about wind instruments. When I make that booming sound I'm always on the wing. I'm going to take a flight now. And when I come back you'll hear a noise that is a noise — and not a squeaky chirp."

Then Mr. Nighthawk left his perch and climbed up into the sky. And when he had risen high enough to suit him he dropped like a stone. It seemed to Chirpy Cricket that he had never heard anything so loud as the boom that broke not far above his head soon afterward. At the very moment when it looked as if Mr. Nighthawk must dash himself to pieces upon the ground, right where Chirpy Cricket crouched and trembled, he had spread his wings and checked his fall. It was the air, rushing through his wing-feathers with great force, that made the queer, hollow sound. That was why Mr. Nighthawk claimed that he made the booming on a wind instrument.

"There!" he said, when he had settled himself in the tree once more. "If you think you can teach me to perform better, just try that trick yourself!"

But Chirpy Cricket said that he was sure Mr. Nighthawk's performance couldn't be bettered by anybody. And he remarked that the noise reminded him of a high wind coming on top of a thunder storm.

That pleased Mr. Nighthawk.

"It's the greatest praise I've ever had!" he declared. And before Chirpy Cricket knew what had happened, Mr. Nighthawk had flown away.

Chirpy often wondered why he left so suddenly. The truth was that Mr. Nighthawk had hurried back to the woods to tell his wife what Chirpy Cricket had said to him. And ever afterward he was fond of repeating Chirpy's remark, in a boasting way, until his neighbors were heartily tired of hearing it.

XXII

HARMLESS MR. MEADOW MOUSE

One night when Chirpy Cricket was fiddling his prettiest, not far from the fence between the farmyard and the meadow, he had a queer feeling, as if somebody were gazing at him. And glancing up quickly, he saw that a plump person sat on a fence-rail, busily engaged in staring at him.

"How-dy do!" Chirpy Cricket piped; for the fat, four-legged person looked both cheerful and harmless. "I take it you're fond of music."

The stranger, whose name was Mr. Meadow Mouse, smiled. "I won't dispute your statement," he said.

"Perhaps you play some instrument yourself," Chirpy observed.

But Mr. Meadow Mouse shook his head.

"No!" he replied. "No! To tell the truth, I haven't much time for that sort of thing. Besides, it seems to me somewhat dangerous. I was wondering, while I watched you, whether you weren't likely to fiddle yourself into bits — you were working so hard."

Chirpy Cricket assured him that there wasn't the least danger.

"All my family are famous fiddlers," he said. "And I've never heard of such an accident happening to any of them."

Mr. Meadow Mouse appeared to be slightly disappointed.

"I thought," he said, "I could pick up the pieces for you, in case you fell apart."

Dark as he was, Chirpy Cricket almost turned pale.

"You — you weren't intending to — to swallow the pieces, were you?" he stammered.

"Dear me! No!" Mr. Meadow Mouse gasped. "I'm what's known as a vegetarian."

Well, when he heard that, Chirpy Cricket made ready to jump out of the stranger's way. He didn't know what a vegetarian was; but it sounded terrible to him.

Mr. Meadow Mouse must have guessed that Chirpy was uneasy. Anyhow, he hastened to explain that a vegetarian was one that ate only food that grew on plants of one kind or another.

"I live for the most part on seeds and grain," he said. "So you see I'm quite harmless."

Chirpy Cricket told him that he was glad to know it.

"I'm a vegetarian myself," he added proudly, "for I eat blades of grass. And you see I'm harmless too."

Mr. Meadow Mouse bestowed another fat smile on him.

"Then," he said, "it must be quite safe for me to stay here and talk with you."

Chirpy Cricket didn't know why the plump gentleman was smiling, unless it was because he felt easy in his mind. Chirpy couldn't help liking him, he was so friendly.

"I'll play my favorite tune for you, if you wish," Chirpy offered, being eager to do something pleasant for his new acquaintance.

"Do!" said Mr. Meadow Mouse. "And make it as lively as you please. For I've just dined well and I'm in a very cheerful mood."

So Chirpy Cricket began his cr-r-r-i! cr-r-r-i! cr-r-r-i! while Mr. Meadow Mouse moved nearer and watched him closely. After a time he began to fidget. And at last he asked Chirpy if he wouldn't please be still for a moment, because there was something he wanted to say.

Chirpy stopped fiddling.

"I notice," said Mr. Meadow Mouse, "that you're having some trouble tuning up your fiddle. So if you don't mind I'll go over in the cornfield on a matter of business and come back here later. Then, no doubt, you'll be all ready to play a tune for me."

Chirpy Cricket had to explain that he had been playing a tune all the time—that he always played on one note.

So Mr. Meadow Mouse stayed and heard more of the fiddling. He begged Chirpy's pardon for his mistake. And he said that if he only had a fiddle he should like to learn the same tune himself. "Although," he added, "it must be very difficult to play always on the same note. It must take a great deal of practice."

XXIII

A WAIL IN THE DARK

There was an odd cry that often interrupted the nightly concerts of the Cricket family. Chirpy Cricket had never heard it in the daytime. But when twilight began to wrap Pleasant Valley in its shadows, the strange, wailing call was almost sure to come quavering through the air. Somehow it always sent a shiver over Chirpy. And sometimes it made him lose a few notes—if he happened to be fiddling when he heard it.

He learned that it was a dangerous bird known as Simon Screecher—a cousin of Solomon Owl—that made this uncanny call. If he had lived, like Solomon, across the meadow in the hemlock woods, Chirpy Cricket would have paid less heed to the noise he made. But Simon Screecher had his home in a hollow apple tree in Farmer Green's orchard.

It was said—by those that claimed to know—that Simon Screecher slept in the daytime. But every tiny night-creature—the Katydids and the Crickets and all the rest—knew that after sunset Simon Screecher was as wide awake as anybody.

It was no wonder that Chirpy Cricket was always uneasy when Simon screeched his warning that he was awake and looking for his supper. Chirpy knew that he could not depend on Simon to stay long in one place. Though you heard his screech in the orchard one moment, you might see him in the farmyard soon afterward. He never ate a whole meal in just one spot, but preferred to move about wherever his fancy took him. Simon himself said that he could eat off and on all night long, if he kept moving.

Somehow Mr. Meadow Mouse had heard of this saying of Simon Screecher's. "You ought to crawl into your hole under the straw whenever Simon Screecher is about the neighborhood," he advised Chirpy one evening, when the two chanced to meet near the fence.

"But Simon is around here every night," Chirpy replied. "If I stayed at home from dusk till dawn I couldn't take part in another concert all summer long."

Mr. Meadow Mouse said that that would be a great pity.

"Don't you suppose"—Chirpy asked him hopefully—"don't you suppose I could jump out of Simon Screecher's reach if he tried to catch me?"

"You could find out by trying," said Mr. Meadow Mouse.

So Chirpy Cricket began to feel more cheerful. He even fiddled a bit, thinking that he had no special reason to worry. And then all at once he stopped making music.

Mr. Meadow Mouse had been searching about on the ground for seeds, while he was enjoying Chirpy's fiddling. And when the music came to a sudden end he looked up and saw that something was troubling the fiddler.

"What's the matter now?" he inquired.

"An unpleasant idea has just come into my head," Chirpy told him. "It would be very unlucky for me if I found that I wasn't spry enough to escape Simon Screecher!"

Mr. Meadow Mouse had to admit that there was a good deal of truth in Chirpy's remark. But he said he was ready with another suggestion. "It's a good one, too," he declared.

"What is it?" Chirpy asked him.

"You'll have to think of some other way"—said Mr. Meadow Mouse—"some other way of being safe from Simon Screecher."

FRIGHTENING SIMON SCREECHER

Mr. Meadow Mouse acted as if he thought he had been a great help when he said that Chirpy Cricket would have to think of another way to avoid Simon Screecher's cruel talons. But the more Chirpy turned the matter over in his mind the further he seemed to be from any plan. For several days and nights he puzzled over his problem. And every time he heard Simon Screecher's unearthly wail he shivered so hard that his fiddling actually seemed to shiver too.

Mr. Meadow Mouse inquired regularly whether Chirpy had hit upon any plan. And at last Mr. Meadow Mouse announced that he would have to think of one himself. So he sat down and looked very wise, while Chirpy Cricket fiddled for him, because Mr. Meadow Mouse explained that his wits always worked better when somebody made music for him.

"Didn't you notice his cry a little while ago?" Mr. Meadow Mouse asked. "Didn't you notice how his voice trembled?"

"Yes!" Chirpy said. "Yes! Now that you speak of it, I remember that his voice shook a good deal."

"Ah!" Mr. Meadow Mouse exclaimed. "Something had frightened him. Now, you had just begun to fiddle before he cried out. And there's no doubt in my mind that your music scared Simon Screecher. So all you need do to feel safe from him is to fiddle a plenty every night."

Chirpy Cricket felt so happy all at once that he began a lively tune. And sure enough! Simon Screecher squalled almost immediately.

"That proves it!" Mr. Meadow Mouse exclaimed. And then he said good evening and ran off to the place where Farmer Green had been threshing oats, feeling very well pleased with himself.

Chirpy Cricket took pains to follow Mr. Meadow Mouse's advice. And neither Simon Screecher — nor his cousin Solomon Owl — troubled Chirpy all the rest of the summer. He fiddled the nights away with more pleasure than ever before. And by the time fall came all his neighbors agreed that he had done even more than his part to make the summer gay for everybody.

THE END